One Special Christmas

NORMA EATON

Paperback-Press
an imprint of A & S Publishing
A & S Holmes, Inc.

ISBN: 0991180526
ISBN-13: 978-0-9911805-2-3

DEDICATION

To my favorite Santa

Art Stone, a Godly man who brings Christmas joy
all year long to those who know him.

You are loved, Art.

CONTENTS

ACKNOWLEDGMENTS

Thanks to my husband Gary for his support and encouragement and sharing the love of God with me. I also give my undying gratitude to my dear talented friend, Sharon Kizziah-Holmes, for all her hard work in helping me get this story published.

CHAPTER 1

*M*eg swallowed the lump in her throat as the taxi pulled up in front of the house she grew up in. She had not been back to Dunsberg since her mother's funeral a couple years ago. The SOLD sign in the yard brought a tear to her eye. She cherished this home and hoped the family who purchased it would love it just as much.

There was a time when she thought she and her now ex-fiancé Richard would come back to live here and raise a family. "Someday," he told her many times, "we will have it all". He told her to be patient, but *all* to her was marriage, children, a comfortable home, but most of all love. Obviously none of those were important to the mighty Richard Travis of Travis-Scott Model Agency.

She shook her head sadly. When he told her New York was where they belonged, she reluctantly agreed to put her childhood home up for sale. After all, as he put it, with his guidance her career as a budding TV star was coming along nicely. Why would they want to move to a back-woods town in Missouri? He said they had prestige, influential contacts, and her being on TV opened a lot of doors in all the right places. She blocked out the rest of the unkind things he said about her beloved hometown.

The taxi driver helped her with her suitcase. "Do you want me to carry it up on the porch, ma'am?"

She smiled when she handed him the fare. "No, I can manage. Thank you." Could she manage though? Yes, she had to. She was on her own and the realization that she was the only person she could depend on had hit hard.

Taking a deep breath, she turned toward the house. The buyers, a minister and his family, wanted to move in before Christmas. That only gave her three weeks to dispose of the rest of her mother's furniture and personal belongings. Oh, she could have hired it all done, but she wanted to come herself. She needed to get out of New York. Needed to feel like her old self. Feel a sense of belonging?

Studying the exterior of the beautiful old place, it looked in good condition. Her mother's trust fund was ample enough for her to have the house looked after until she could move back or—she choked back a sob. She could barely even think the words, sold it, but it was too late. She had to accept she'd never live here again.

"Meggie!!"

She turned and saw her old neighbor, Art. His long white beard ruffled in the wind as he ran toward her. He was the town's Santa and all the kids flocked around him even when he was not wearing his Santa suit. As a kid, she had been no exception. It seemed a lifetime ago.

"Art." She fell into his embrace. "I need to be drinking the same water as you. You haven't aged one bit."

"And look at you." He pushed her back to arm's length. "You're even prettier than you were when you left here. You still got those baby blues and beautiful blond curls. I see you on TV all the time. I almost bought that shampoo you advertised to make my hair shine." He took off his hat to reveal his baldhead.

Meg laughed. Art always had the ability to make her smile. She tugged at his whiskers "You could have used it on your beard."

"I suppose." He pointed toward her house. "I've tried to keep it in tip-top shape since your mama's passing and the Mrs. put fresh linens on your bed. We presumed you'd be staying a few days at least."

She nodded. "I need to make arrangements to auction off the furniture to get the house ready for the new occupants."

"I can help with anything you need," he offered. Then just before he turned to go back home, he added, "I fixed up that old tree house in the back yard. It's kind of cold right now, but this spring, those little kids moving in will love to play there. Just like you used to when you were a tyke." His eyes misted. "I remember finding you up there right after your daddy died, crying your eyes out."

She smiled remembering how the older man had hugged her and tried to soothe her grief. "That was a sad time for me and Mom."

"No better folks, your mama and daddy. Good, Godly people."

Godly? She knew down deep they were, but God had forsaken her. She cleared her throat. "Thanks for everything. I hope my mother's lawyers have compensated you well for your work."

"They surely have, Meggie, but I'd have done it for nothin'. That's God's way. Do unto others as you would have—"

"I need to get inside, Art." She didn't mean to sound so harsh, but she also didn't want to hear about "*God's way*".

"Yell if you need anything," he called out as she hurried up the front steps. He raised his voice, "I also had the chimney cleaned. Don't want to get dirty when I come down it Christmas Eve." He chuckled. "If you haven't told Santa what you want for Christmas, I'll be at the mall tomorrow."

She didn't look at him when she placed the key in the lock and turned it "I quit believing in Santa a long time ago."

"No one quits believin', Meggie."

She pretended not to hear and let herself into the house. If he only knew the things she'd been through, he might understand. Pulling her bag inside, she thought about Richard and his betrayal.

She had felt a strain between them and had considered breaking off their engagement herself, but she wouldn't have just left town like he did. Especially not with the expensive paintings they'd collected together. She would have at least talked to him about it.

The coward couldn't even tell her face to face he was leaving. The words of the note he left on her kitchen table still stung. *It's just not working for me.* However, the worst of it all was that he had taken *Cynthia*, the new model in his agency, with him.

She closed the door behind her and inhaled the familiar smell of home. Why was she letting Richard dominate her thoughts? She had more important things to do, and starting now, she was going to try to enjoy the time she had left in her home.

Everything appeared to be in pristine condition as she glanced around the living room. It looked just like when she was here for her mother's funeral. Sadness engulfed her. She missed her mother. She would have loved to have her here to talk to, to hug.

This was her home, she ran her hand along the fireplace mantle and thought of the many Christmas mornings she'd ran down the stairs to see what was under the tree. She'd dreamed of raising her own kids here. She would have loved for them to be carefree and happy just as she was. Kids? That's not happening, she told herself.

Art's lovely wife, Barbara, had stocked the refrigerator with sandwich makings and fruit. Meg made herself a snack and a cup of tea, pondering what to do with all the things she had grown up with.

Tired, she went upstairs to her old room and marveled how nothing had changed. Her high school posters were still on the wall. Volleyball trophies sat on the shelf above the headboard. Her old Raggedy Ann doll nestled against the pillows, waiting for her to come lie down with her. She crumpled to the bed, pulled the doll into her arms, and sobbed herself to sleep.

CHAPTER 2

*H*er cell phone ringing woke her early the next morning. She frowned when she saw Richard's partner Bart Scott's name on the caller ID.

"Yes?" she answered.

"How long you going to be out of civilization?"

That rankled her. The remark reminded her of the disparaging remarks Richard used to make about her hometown. "As long as it takes," she said curtly. "As a matter of fact, cancel all of my engagements until you hear from me." She heard her agent's raspy breath escape and wished she hadn't answered.

"You know what this will do to your career? Not to mention, when you don't work, I don't get paid. Are you crazy? Get yourself back here pronto!"

"Get myself back there?" Who did he think he was? "I'll do no such thing. Not until I feel like it." Her career was never her idea. Richard had pushed her into it for the "prestige" and what money he could make off her. She saw that now and it hurt that she was so stupid to go along with everything.

"Listen, Missy. Richard and I had a deal that he would see you showed for the audition he set up for a spot on a soap. If you don't come back on the next flight, you can kiss your career goodbye. I'll see you never work in this town again."

"What? You had a deal with Richard? Well, I thought Richard had a deal with me, too. See how that worked out." She had lost more than her career, and at this point, she could care less. "Tell you what. You get hold of that deal-making slime ball, if you can find him, and maybe his *new* money-maker will be more to your liking. She's much more sophisticated."

"And more accommodating, I would imagine."

"What is that supposed to mean?"

"Staying 'pure' until marriage? What kind of back-woods thinking is that in this day and age? How old are you, twenty-seven, eight? And still a virgin?" He laughed. "What a loser. Richard was right. You can take the hick out of Hicksville, but you can't take Hicksville—"

"How dare he discuss our personal matters with you! That was …oh, why should I explain anything to you."

Richard had acted like he respected her wishes to wait until marriage to consummate their love. Now she knew he'd been with other women throughout their four-year relationship and it made her sick to her stomach. How could she have been so blind!

"She almost burst into angry tears but choked them back. "By the way, if you do talk to Mr.

Slime, tell him I want my half of what he stole from my apartment or I will have my 'hick' police friends track him down like a dog. Do I make myself clear?"

"You know we can sue you, don't you?" Bart said snidely.

She was silent for a moment. *Sue her*?

"I thought that might get your attention." He laughed.

"For what?"

"Breach of contract."

"As the saying goes," she said, not wanting to show she cared what he did, "don't call me, I'll call you." She closed the phone and threw it across the bed. If she never saw *"civilization"* again, it would suit her just fine. She was having a childish snit and knew it, but it felt good to air her feelings instead of being the puppet she had become to please Richard.

****

She had just finished showering and dressing when the doorbell rang. It was Santa in his suit, and Mrs. Santa in hers, with a plate of warm cinnamon rolls.

"You guys." She smiled and inhaled the yummy aroma of the pastry. "You didn't have to do this. I was about to go out for some packing supplies and could have gotten some breakfast."

Mrs. Santa stepped inside and gave her a hug. "We're on our way to the mall and thought maybe you'd join us and watch the kids sit on Santa's lap. It's at the top of the *cuteness* scale, you know."

She nodded. "You go on. I'll catch up with you later, after I've run my errands." She took the plate of rolls from Art. "And after I gobble up some of these luscious morsels." She kissed them each on the cheek, then gave a two-fingered wave and watched them walk hand in hand back to their old pickup truck, giggling like a couple of teenagers. Oh how she used to love to ride in the back of that old truck and let the wind blow her to pieces. Again, another lifetime, she thought sadly.

She called a nearby service station, that used to have rentals, and lucked out on an SUV to use for a couple of weeks. "Could you deliver it to me? I'd be glad to pay extra."

"No problem. What's the address?"

"Do you remember Ada Stanley's place?"

There was a brief pause. "Is this by any chance Megan Stanley?"

"Yes, who's this?"

"Brian. Brian Stokes. I was in your English class. I heard the preacher bought your mom's house."

"Oh, for heaven's sake. Brian, it's nice to hear your voice. It's been a long time." She thought for a moment. "Of course, I just noticed the name in the phone book that I'm calling. Stokes Automotive. Your dad's company."

"Well, dad passed away shortly after your mother. It's just me and a couple hired hands now."

"Sorry." It saddened her heart that the older generation, the people she knew and loved, were beginning to pass.

"Yeah, hard to be a kid when you lose your

parents. I guess we all have to grow up. I got three kids now. You?"

Another stab to the heart. Kids. "No, never married."

"How long you here for?"

"Don't know for sure. At least until I get all the loose ends around here tied up." She glanced at her watch. "Can you bring the car over soon? I have a lot of errands to run."

"Be right there."

It was good to see someone from her high school days, and she vowed they would get together for coffee so she could meet his wife and kids before she left. Left? For where, she thought glumly. She would have to go back and take care of the lease on the apartment if nothing else. She mentally thanked her mom for insisting she get a teacher's degree. At least, if she would never have children of her own, she could teach other people's children.

****

Errands run, boxes loaded in the back of the SUV, she walked into the mall just in time to see two adorable children, a boy and his younger sister, climb on Santa's lap.

"Ho, ho, ho," said Santa. "You must be Charlie and Katy."

Their eyes widened. "How'd you know?" Charlie asked.

"I'm Santa. I know things."

"Like who's been naughty and nice?" The boy grinned.

"Exactly. Have you two been nice?"

Charlie nodded but Katy shrugged her shoulders. "Sometimes Charlie calls me stupid and dad says that's not nice."

Santa gave Charlie the eye and the boy quickly whispered loudly, "I don't do that anymore."

"Well, then, I guess you might as well tell me what you want for Christmas and we'll see what we can do."

Meg was almost laughing and crying at the same time. These children were so adorable.

"Well," Charlie started, "we want you to bring our dad another nice lady for him to love. He's really lonely since our mother died."

That did it. Meg couldn't stop the tears that streamed down her cheeks. Their mother died? How sad!

"And, and, and," Katy chimed in, "make her like kids like our mommy did. She has to like hugs and telling bedtime stories."

"Uh, huh, I see," Santa said. "Anything else?"

Charlie leaned in close to Santa. "It wouldn't hurt if she could make pecan pie. Dad loves pecan pie. He said he could eat his weight in pecan pie."

Katy added, "It would be nice if she was pretty. Our mommy was pretty."

The little dark haired girl glanced at the audience standing around in awe of them. Meg included, couldn't believe what these children were asking Santa for.

"Kind of like that lady." She pointed toward the crowd.

Meg's heart stopped the moment it dawned on

her the girl was pointing at her.

Santa nodded. "That certainly is a pretty lady." He smiled at Meg. "You've given me a pretty big order, but I'll see what I can do. Can't promise for sure."

Katy patted Santa's cheek. "You can do it, Santa. I've prayed for God to help you."

"That's the best helper anyone could have, Katy, and thank you for mentioning me to Him." Santa was talking to Katy, but his eyes were on Meg. "God can help everyone. All you need to do is ask."

Meg turned and ran out of the mall. Maybe for some people, but not for her. What good would it do her to ask God for help? Waste of breath.

CHAPTER 3

After picking up some take-out food and a few groceries at the Shop and Go, Meg went home to start packing. She needed to get her mind off those children. It was too heartbreaking to know they lost their mother at such a young age.

One bite of her supper was all she got down before the doorbell rang. She let her breath out in exasperation. "Who now?" Santa and Mrs. Santa stood beaming at her.

"Come to church with us and meet the new pastor who bought your house."

"Art, thanks but I don't go to church anymore."

He frowned. "And why is that? You never missed Sunday school and church. Why would a Wednesday evening be any different?"

She hesitated, but decided to tell the truth. "I feel abandoned by God."

"Oh, Meggie, God does not abandon anyone."

"Well, he has me. I prayed to Him for years over

things that really mattered to me. All I got was a broken heart. He never answered one of those prayers."

"Meggie, Meggie." Barbara put her arms around Meg's shoulders. "God doesn't always give you what you ask for, but he'll always give you what you need." She stood back and wiped a tear from Meg's cheek with her thumb. "Now, come with us. I'll not take no for an answer."

Meg had always loved Art and Barbara and couldn't make herself disappoint them anymore than she had, so she reluctantly grabbed her coat and offered to drive them in her rented SUV.

****

It looked like new paint on the walls of the church and maybe new pew covers, but the beautiful stained glass window she loved as a youth was still there. Even after all these years, she felt her parents' presence. They were always so active in church doings. Those were good times, but that was another lifetime. This was real time and church had not been a part of her life since she and Richard had, had—had what? Become a twosome? Thinking back, she didn't know what to call their relationship.

She saw the two children from the mall running toward her. They wrapped their arms around her legs and waist. "Oh, thank you, Santa."

Embarrassed, Meg looked to Art for support. He shrugged. He obviously had nothing to say. "Children," She wiggled from their embraces ."I'm just here to meet the new preacher. He bought my mother's house." She missed the warmth of the little ones' hugs as soon as they let her go.

"That's our Daddy!"

She heard them shout in unison. She turned to Art and gave him the evil eye. "You knew who these children were at the mall, didn't you?" Art gave her his best Santa smile, and she knew what he was up to. Just then a tall handsome, vaguely familiar, man in a robe sauntered down the aisle. His deep voice was kind when he spoke.

"Kids go to your seats now and leave this lady alone."

Charlie stepped forward. "But, Dad, this is her. The lady from the mall we told you about."

"Go. Sit." He pointed to one of the pews.

Turning to Meg, he leaned in close. "Sorry about that, Megan. I had no idea it was you they were talking about."

She frowned and stepped back to get a better look at his face. She had seen him before, but where? "Do I know you?" No one called her Megan since school days.

"I was a couple of years ahead of you at Dunsberg High. Then I went off to college and seminary and you went to God knows where. When I saw your old house for sale, I had to buy it. I always loved that house and it's perfect to raise my kids in."

That's exactly what *she* had thought all of her adult life. "Yes, it's a great house for a family." She couldn't take her eyes off of him.

"I was hoping I'd get to see you. We need to

catch up on old times."

She gave him a puzzling, clueless look. Old times? Whoever he was, she knew she'd never really spent any time with him, so how could they catch up?

"I've seen you in commercials. You're a natural." He put his hand out. "Anthony Stenbrook. Please don't destroy my ego completely by not remembering me," he said with a chuckle.

Her mouth dropped open as realization dawned. "Tony? Tony, star basketball player, the most popular boy in your class Tony?" She started giggling and punched him lightly on his shoulder. "Of course I remember you. I just didn't recognize you out of your basketball shorts."

That remark made him raise one eyebrow and smile. He was so cute! Looking him up and down, she shook her head in amazement. "It really is you"

"Last time I looked in the mirror, it was really me."

"I just can't believe it. A preacher. The same guy all of us girls had a major crush on. I always thought you'd go pro."

"Thanks for your vote of confidence, and for the major crush thing, but I wanted more. I wanted what God wanted for me. I wanted a family to love and a venue to help guide others to the Lord. When the former pastor here retired, I knew it was Devine intervention for me to move back here, to be close to my parents, and to pastor this church. In fact, we're staying with my folks until your house is ready for us to move into."

"Mr. and Mrs. Stenbrook," Meg said

nostalgically. "I will always be grateful to them for the kindness they showed my mother and me when dad died." She looked up at him and smiled. "You, too, Tony. You were so sweet to mow Mom's yard and trim her bushes all that summer."

"Yeah, I remember that. Tough times. Sorry about your mom, too."

"You're right. Tough times." She looked up into dark brown eyes full of compassion. "Speaking of tough times. I overheard your kids talking to Santa about their mother –"

He held his hand up to stop her. "We know she's in a better place, and we will always miss her. She was a great lady, but she's with God and He's got another angel in his flock."

God again. Will He never quit pestering her conscience? She looked around. "Are your folks here? I'd like to say hi."

"No, they're out of town visiting Mom's sister. They'll be back in a few days. Come," he said taking her elbow to escort her to a seat, "sit here with the kids. I know they would love it. Do you like to sing?"

"I like to, but I don't know if others like listening to me," she said with a chuckle.

"God says to make a joyful noise."

He handed her a hymnal and walked to the pulpit. When he smiled at her and she felt her heart flutter. Oh, no.

"Please turn to page 265 and, let's make a joyful noise."

He still had that drop-dead grin and those straight white-as-snow teeth. She had worn braces when she was young and her teeth were not as straight as his. And those dark eyes!! Eyes that used to make her and her girlfriends melt down to their socks. She should be ashamed. What was wrong with her? That was also in that other lifetime.

After the singing of several hymns and then a powerful sermon that surprised her at its intensity, Tony announced there would be refreshments in the basement and Santa would hand out treats to kids of all ages.

After the festivities, she couldn't remember when she had such a happy time. Charlie and Katy never left her side and she relished in their antics, laughing so much her sides ached.

When it was time to go, she complimented Tony on his sermon and told him how delightful his children are. As she turned to leave, he took hold of her hand.

"Hey, do you think the kids and I could take you out for a burger or something? Maybe you could help them pick out a gift for their grandma. I got Dad a new chain saw but have no clue what to get Mom."

She thought for a moment. It was a tempting offer, but she wasn't ready. Not yet. "I'm not in a good place in my life right now, Tony." She pulled her hand from his. "It has nothing to do with you. It's been delightful spending the evening with the kids, but I just..." His eyes were kind and understanding when she met his gaze.

"It's fine. I'm sorry you're having a bad time. We'll pray for you."

She glanced down. "That won't do any good."

Turning, she joined Art and Barbara, but felt him staring at her as she and her neighbors walked out the door.

CHAPTER 4

"Cute kids, huh?" Art said as they pulled into her driveway.

"Stop it, Art," Barbara scolded. "I know what you're doing? You're playing match-maker again."

"I'm just saying, I think the kids are cute."

"I know what you're saying. I've lived with you over fifty years. You're saying, those kids sure liked you, Meg. You and Tony make a swell couple."

"Oh, shush, Barbara. I'm not saying any such thing. Meg's a big girl now. She can come to her own conclusions."

He winked at Meg, and that Santa twinkle shone brightly in the moonlight.

"Night, Santa. She kissed him on the cheek and gave him a shove out of the car.

****

Meg lay in bed and stared at the full moon out

her window. She had to admit, Art was right, those kids were exceptionally cute. She thought of their dad. She remembered him, from school days, being so nice to everyone. That was a lot of his appeal with the girls. He never flirted or anything but he had a way of looking at you that could make you smile for a week. She felt some of that tonight when she looked into his eyes.

Stop it!!! *I'm here on a mission, then back to New York to rid myself of that life, then decide where I will live and try to get a teaching job.* She would love for her new life to be here, but that just wouldn't work. Those kids want a Momma and a wife for their dad and they'd picked her. It wouldn't be fair to them. She had a shattered heart to mend before she could let anyone in again. Maybe that would never happen.

Sleep came easily despite all the jumbled thoughts running through her mind. She rose early and started her work. Packing was going along as well as it could, though her heart wasn't in it. She needed a break.

The sun was out and the day was somewhat warmer than it had been so she took her afternoon cup of tea out on the front porch to enjoy the day. She had just settled in the chaise when she heard two boisterous voices coming from Art and Barbara's yard.

"Santa, come out and play catch with us."

It was Charlie, and she couldn't help but smile when she saw Katy skipping toward Art's porch. Then Katy turned around, she saw her and waved. She went up on her tiptoes and walked stealthily toward Meg, and whispered loudly.

"Dad said we were not to bother you." She put her finger to her lips. "Shhh, am I bothering you?"

Meg smiled. "Of course not. Where's your Dad? And why aren't you in school?"

"Furnace broke. We don't have to go back until they fix it and Dad's in Santa's house. He wants Santa to go help him find a big Christmas tree that we can cut down and let Santa haul it in his truck. Dad said we could ride in the back with the tree. Won't that be grand? I've never got to ride in the back of a truck."

Memories ran through her mind. "I have, and it *is* grand."

"When we move into your house, that tree will be the biggest, most beautiful tree in the whole wide world. Do you want to help decorate it?"

"Sorry, sweetie, but I won't be here when you move into this house. It will be your house then."

Katy's bottom lip drooped down. "Why? Why can't it be your house, too?"

Meg couldn't take it any longer. She reached out to Katy and took her on her lap. This is what she was afraid of. Attachment. "Honey, someday a new mommy will come along and you'll be so happy. She'll love hugs, kisses and telling bedtime stories. She'll love your daddy with all her heart and life will be so joyful and carefree. There will be lots fun and games and no more tears."

Her heart skipped a beat. She was describing what her dream life was supposed to be before Mr. Richard, the womanizing jerk-face, took four years of her life and turned her into a distrustful, bitter person incapable of loving, and afraid to be loved by anyone.

She helped the little girl down from her lap. "You'd better go back to Santa's house, Honey, before your Dad finds you here. We don't want to get into trouble."

Katy wiped her nose upward with her hand. "I love you, Meg."

A large lump formed in Meg's throat. "Sweetie, you hardly know me."

"God knows you. He sent you to us. He told Santa to find you and he did. Dad says God puts love in our hearts so we can give it to others. God will put love in your heart and you will love us." With that she turned and skipped across to Art's house.

Meg could only stare after her. How could one so young be so loving and trustful and...she couldn't think of the word but Godly came to mind.

****

Two days later just before she was going to call an auction house about the furniture, Tony, the kids and his parents came to the house. They brought enough food for an army and wanted to talk.

"Of course, come in." She took plates and bowls from them into the kitchen. "It is so nice to see you Mr. and Mrs. Stenbrook. I hope you had a nice trip."

"It was lovely, Megan. We've looked forward to seeing you again, too. The kids talk about you incessantly. You really made an impression on them."

"I don't know what I did, but I'm flattered. They're darling children." Charlie and Katy both hugged her and she returned the embrace. "How was school today?" They shook their head no. "Furnace still broken?"

Tony put a cake on the table. "The school is having major problems with their heating system, and since it is so close to shut down for Christmas vacation, they may not go back until after the first of the year."

Meg smiled at the children. "Yea for you, huh?"

Mrs. Stenbrook stepped forward. "We come to not only share dinner with you but to ask a big favor."

Meg raised her brows. What kind of favor could they possibly want from her? "Sure. What can I do for you?"

"Well, we know you're going to auction off the furniture, so we'd like to buy it for Tony. Sort of a Christmas gift to him and the children. We'll, of course, give you a very fair price. It would be so much easier than him having to buy new before Christmas. He didn't keep any of his household." She leaned forward and whispered in Meg's ear. "I think he wanted to make a new start."

"No problem. We can do that." Meg was relieved that she wouldn't have to see it go to strangers. It was like a prayer answered. No, that couldn't be. It was a coincidence.

"Another thing is, we…well, the children, wanted to know if they could put their Christmas tree up early. "

Meg opened her mouth to say something but Mrs. Stenbrook held her hand up.

"I know it's an imposition before the closing on the house, but it's Christmas in a couple of weeks and a big tree is all Charlie and Katy have been talking about."

Meg looked around the large living room. "Well, I guess we could move the couch over there near the entry and make room for the tree in front of the window." She looked at everyone. "I presume you want to see it from the street. We always did when I was a child."

They all, including Mr. Stenbrook, came together with her for a group hug. She saw Tony's lips form, "Thank you so much."

After stuffing themselves with all the food Mrs. Stenbrook brought and moving furniture around, they decided they needed a good night's rest and tomorrow afternoon would be a good time to bring the tree in. It was still in the back of Art's truck. The kids and grandparents walked out but Tony turned to her before leaving.

"We need to talk," he said softly.

Meg breathed in deeply. "Tony, if it's about us." Us? Why would she even say that? There wasn't an... us to talk about. Now she felt stupid for even thinking it, much less saying it out loud.

"No, Meg. I want to talk to you as your pastor and friend."

She raised her brows and shot him a questioning glance. As her pastor? She wasn't a member of his church, why would he care.

"Art told me he thought something must have

happened to you in New York that—how did he put it—'broke your heart and took some of your sparkle away'."

She laughed snidely. "Sparkle? Ya think?" She silently counted to ten and calmed herself. Tony didn't deserve to be talked to that way. "I shouldn't have used that tone. Art worries too much. Yes, I had some troubles but it's something I can take care of myself."

"But you don't have to be alone in this. You have friends. You have God."

"Please, Tony, I don't want to be disrespectful, but God is not in my life anymore, and hasn't been for quite some time. Now, please, go, your family's waiting."

He reached for her and wrapped his arms around her, his hand sliding softly over her hair. She liked the way his embrace felt. Safe and caring.

"I think you need a friendly hug."

She felt she was floating in a sea of warm water, and for an instant, the warmth lulled her into a dream-like state. Tony's deep voice penetrated her thoughts.

"God is always in our lives, even if we can't see Him. He doesn't close a door without opening another. That's your pastor speaking." He breathed in. "This is your friend talking now. Did you love him?"

Startled at his question, she looked up at him. "Who?"

"Him. There's always a him, or her, when a broken heart is in the picture."

She reluctantly pulled away unsure of how to

answer. Had she ever really been in love with Richard? She'd never felt safe in his embrace like she did only moments ago in Tony's. "Love?" She shook her head and shrugged. "I'm not sure I know what love is anymore. I did everything he asked, but it wasn't enough. It was never going to be enough. I know that now."

"He's an idiot."

She almost laughed out loud. "Is this my pastor speaking or my friend?"

"Neither. Just an outsider's manly observation. Ever since I met you in high school, I thought you were one of the nicest girls I knew."

"Hmmmm, then how come you never said anything to me back then?"

"I'm an idiot."

This time she did laugh out loud. "Another manly observation?"

He gently tapped her on the end of her nose. "Something like that." In an instant, he turned, walked out then closed the door.

CHAPTER 5

$\mathcal{S}$he spent a good portion of the night staring at the ceiling. What was happening? She had felt so good in his arms and he, no doubt, could still make her weak in the knees just by looking at her. No way this was real. She was just living in the past, remembering high school days when she and her girlfriends ogled over the older boys on the basketball team.

This was now. She was still hurt from being dumped by the "*idiot*", and self-sabotaging her career, not to mention having no place to call home anymore. Feeling weak-kneed over a man had no place in her life right now.

Frustrated, she turned over and pulled the blanket over her head, hoping not to dream about the tall, dark preacher man...or maybe wishing she would. "I'm the idiot," she whispered before she drifted off to sleep.

****

The next afternoon, the house was filled with a lot of primal grunts while Meg and Tony pulled on the huge tree to get it through the front doorway without breaking its limbs or scratching the paint on the door.

Meg stood back and placed her hands on her hips. Laughter bubbled up inside her and found its way out. "Couldn't you find any bigger tree? I hate skimpy Christmas trees."

That made the children giggle and Katy asked, "Santa helped Dad make a stand for it. As soon as we get it up, will you go to the mall and help us pick out decorations?"

Her heart strings were already being tightened by the little ones, she didn't want them to get any tighter by spending more time with them then she had to. "Oh, no. That should be something you do yourselves. You can make it your own special tree." Katy did the hanging-lip thing and Charlie whined, "Please, please, please."

"Where's Santa when we need him?" Meg asked.

"He's at the mall already seeing what kids want for Christmas again. He's going to be there every day until Christmas. He has lots and lots of kids to talk to, he said. He doesn't have time to shop for decorations," Charlie explained, still looking at her with pleading eyes.

"I'd welcome the company," Tony added, smiling.

She looked at him. "Where are your parents?"

"Dad wasn't feeling well and Mom said she needed to tend to him."

Sighing, Meg relented while all the time in the back of her mind thinking it was a mistake. "Okay, let's get this monster tree standing while we still have a little strength left. Then it's off to the mall we go."

Squeals of delight echoed through the room and she thought one of those squeals might have come from Tony.

****

The weather had turned cold again and they all bundled up for their trek across the mall's parking lot. Shoppers were out in full force as she and Tony tried to keep up with the kids as they scampered through the crowd.

Finally arriving at the section of decorations and lights, Charlie and Katy ooohed and aaahed and picked first one thing, then another that caught their eye.

"How much are you planning on getting?" Meg asked.

"Well," Tony replied, "you said you didn't like a skimpy tree—so I guess as much as it takes to cover it." He picked up four strings of lights and several boxes of tinsel.

Charlie loaded his arms with boxes of blue and red balls and Katy had her hands full of plastic stars. Meg looked around, spied an empty cart and brought it to them. "Looks like we're going to need this."

They filled the cart with their selections and then Katy's lip dropped again.

"What's wrong, sweetie?" Tony asked.

"Where's the angel?"

"Angel?"

"God's helper. The angel for the top of the tree who looks over us and keeps us safe."

Tony picked his little girl up. "Daddy doesn't see any at this store. Maybe we can find one somewhere else." He wiped a tear from Katy's cheek. "Don't cry, baby, we'll get one somewhere."

The scene almost broke Meg's heart, then she remembered the large angel her mother always had at the top of their trees. It must still be in the attic. She had not gotten up there with her packing efforts yet. "I might know where one is." She looked at Katy's tearful eyes and her heart melted. "I think there is an angel that comes with the house you bought. Let's go home and see if we can find her."

Katy smiled broadly as Tony put her down. "Did she look after you when you lived there?"

Meg couldn't tell Katy she had lost faith in such things. The child was so full of innocence. "I, I'm sure someone looked after me."

Katy and Charlie both nodded and Charlie said, "It was the angel. They do those kinds of things."

"Mommy is an angel now," Katy added.

That brought a tear to Meg's eyes and Tony put his arm around her shoulders.

"Let's pay for this loot, grab a couple huge pizzas and go back to the house, do some major decorating and eat ourselves into a coma. I'm starving!"

****

Major decorating and coma eating lasted to nearly midnight for Meg and Tony. The kids fizzled out around ten thirty and were asleep on the couch.

"I'm going to try to find the angel now."

"Okay." Tony put the last ornament on the tree. "Need help."

"No, I'll be fine." Meg went to the attic and it didn't take long to find the angel. She was surprised it was in such good condition. "Mom." She smiled to herself and spoke into thin air, "Mom always kept everything like new." Her eye caught a small box on an old chair and opened it. She smiled again, it was her mom's recipes. She missed her mother's marvelous dishes she used to make. Putting the box under her arm, she thought maybe she'd make some of her favorites before she left town. She closed the attic door and made her way back down stairs. She held the tree topper out.

"You found it?" Tony said, taking the angel from her. "She's beautiful. The kids will simply love her."

Meg deposited the box of recipes on a nearby table and told Tony to hold the stepladder still while she climbed up to put the angel on the top.

He helped her down and held her just a little longer than necessary, but she found herself not minding at all. Clearing her throat and reluctantly pulling away, she gestured toward the children. "Why don't you leave them here for the night. It's too cold to wake them. I'll get a blanket for Charlie and you can carry Katy up to my room. She can sleep there with me. I wouldn't want her to wake up and be scared. Charlie will be okay here, won't he?"

"Oh, yeah, Charlie would know where he is if he wakes before morning. Thanks, Meg. Good idea. I've still got Art's truck. He and Barbara used her car today and I'll need to get his truck back to him tomorrow somehow."

"Tell you what? Since your dad's not feeling well, there's no need for your parents to follow you over here. Come for breakfast and then I'll drive you and the kids back to your house."

Tony gazed into her eyes. "You're something, Meg Stanley."

"Something?" Was he flirting with her? His perusal made tingles dance down her arms. Hmmm, this was something she'd never experienced before.

"Amazing may be a better word. I feel like I've known you all my life."

"Well, actually you *have* known me for a good part of your life."

He stepped closer and pulled her into his embrace. "Not long enough."

Warm water again. She couldn't understand it but a peace came over her. She felt calm and sheltered.

"Gotta go." He pulled away. "I'd better get Katy upstairs." He lifted the child into his arms.

"First door on the left," Meg said.

"That's the one Katy picked out for her own when we looked at the house to buy. The one with the Raggedy Ann doll?"

Meg nodded, then followed him up the stairs and

helped him pull Katy's shoes and socks off. She tucked the doll under Katy's arm and nestled the girl under the covers.

"I'll see you in the morning," Tony whispered. "I'll see myself out and lock your door. Thanks for babysitting."

"My pleasure. Oh, here's a blanket to cover Charlie with." She handed him the cover from the closet shelf and their hands touched and lingered a long minute. With one finger he tilted her chin up and pressed his lips lightly on hers. Tingles where not only dancing down her arms, but all over her body.

"I hope that didn't offend you, Meg. I just wanted to thank you for all you've done to make these last few days so enjoyable for the kids and me. I was afraid Christmas was going to be hard on them this year with a new school, new home–"

"No offense taken." She stood stunned as he turned and left the room. Moments later she heard the front door close and lock. She put her fingers to her lips, still feeling the impact of his tender kiss.

CHAPTER 6

$\mathcal{M}$eg woke with Katy snuggled against her, Raggedy clutched in her small hand. She hated to move. A child's little body so warm and soft against her back felt like heaven. What was happening? She could not let herself get attached to these children, but she was afraid it had already happened.

Meg gently shook Katy's shoulder. "Sweetie, time to wake up."

The little girl stirred and stretched. When her eyes opened, she looked around then smiled broadly. "Did I sleep here all night?"

"You did. You slept with me. Kind of a slumber party."

"What's a slumber party?"

"That's when friends have a sleep over with other friends. Charlie's asleep on the couch downstairs."

Katy scrambled out of bed and picked up her shoes and socks in one hand but held on tight to

Raggedy Ann. "I need to tell Charlie we had a slumber party."

Meg raced down the stairs trying to keep up with the tyke. "If your brother's still sleeping, don't wake him."

"Where's my dad?" Katy looked around the living room.

"He went home last night."

"Why didn't he stay and have a slumber party? He's your friend, too? I heard him tell Grandma he really liked you."

"Uh, well, uh, I think he had other things to do," quickly adding, "Let's start breakfast. Do you like French toast?" She started for the kitchen, still pondering on their father telling his mom he really liked her. For a scant second she wondered if it could work, but she shot the idea down as fast as it came to mind. Men were not trustworthy, no matter who they were, she couldn't forget that.

"We love French toast," Katy squealed, jumping up and down. "Charlie, Meg is fixing French toast." She woke her brother by landing on top of him.

Meg pulled the eggs out of the fridge. She wondered if the boy would retaliate for being so abruptly brought out of his slumber. She laughed to herself when she heard Charlie's sleepy voice.

"If Dad ever has another kid, I hope it's not a girl."

"That's not very nice."

"Oh be quiet you little pest."

"Meg, Charlie called me a pest!"

She smiled at their banter. "Okay, you two, that's enough. Go wash up for breakfast." Then she heard Charlie speak again, this time his voice held something akin to awe.

"Look, Katy. I told you a beautiful angel would watch over us." Walking into the living room, Meg wiped her hands on a towel. She wanted to see the children's faces. Little Katy's eyes were opened wide and so were her brother's. She had probably looked at that angel the same way hundreds of times over the years. Now she knew how her mother felt, and her heart soared.

"Wow. She's so pretty. Can we turn on the lights?" Katy ran to where the plug lay on the floor.

"I'll do it for you," Meg offered and when she plugged them in, it illuminated the entire room and the angel's eyes shone brightly as she gazed down on her new family.

****

French toast keeping warm in the oven and eggs whipped ready to be scrambled, Meg had the kids help her stem strawberries while she made homemade syrup for the toast. She felt happy. This was what she was meant to do. Make breakfast while listening to happy kids bickering over who was doing the best job.

"You're both doing great. Now wash the berries again and put them in this bowl. I'll sprinkle some sugar on them to make them sweet." She grabbed both kids and kissed each on their cheeks. "Almost as sweet as you two." Charlie blushed and Katy giggled.

When the doorbell rang, they were still giggling

and chasing each other around the kitchen.

"I think your Dad's here." Meg went to the door and when she opened it, her heart stood still for a moment. She found it hard to believe how much she looked forward to seeing him.

"What's all the racket?" Tony stepped inside.. "I could hear a lot of noise outside the door."

Katy ran to him and jumped into his arms. "We had a slumber party, Daddy. It was fun."

"How'd you like it, Charlie?" Tony ruffled the boy's hair.

"It was cool. You get to sleep in your clothes." When Tony and Meg laughed, the boy asked, "Isn't that what a slumber party is?"

"No, silly." Katy butted in. "It's when friends sleep over at their friend's house."

"Duh." Charlie swiped at his wrinkled shirt. "I know that. Sleeping at a friend's house…in your clothes."

Katy looked at her dad. "Why didn't you stay over, Daddy. You said you liked Meg. She's your friend, too."

Tony rolled his eyes and Meg recognized his plea for help. "She already asked me that. You take it from here."

"Well, I, uh, I don't like sleeping in my clothes?"

Meg couldn't help herself. She broke into full laughter as she headed to the kitchen to finish up breakfast. She watched Katy pull up a chair next to her at the table for Raggedy Ann and Meg put a small plate in front of the doll, just like her mother used to do. Raggedy had been a big part of her childhood and she felt it was time she let the doll find a new friend to love her.

"I think Raggedy likes you." She picked up the doll, straightened her dress then sat her back in the chair. "Would you like to keep her?"

"Really?"

The happiness in the little one's voice almost made her tear up, but she blinked back the emotion. "Yes, really."

"Oh, thank you, Meg." Katy hugged her then promptly kissed the doll on top of her head. "She's my friend. We had a slumber party together."

"And you both slept in your clothes," Charlie added smartly.

****

While the kids were putting more tinsel on the tree, Tony helped Meg clean up the kitchen. While at the sink, he put his hand over hers. "Thanks, again. I haven't seen the kids this happy in a long time."

"Look at me. I haven't seen myself this happy in a long time." This time her emotion spilled over and tears did well in her eyes. "Your children are special. I guess you know that."

"They are, and so are you." He squeezed her hand tighter. "I just can't believe a man could give you up."

"I guess the grass was greener in another pasture."

"You mean he left you for another woman?"

"A more *accommodating* one. I told you, I wasn't good enough."

"Don't do that to yourself. You're not only good enough, you're better than most. He doesn't deserve forgiveness from you for what he did, but you need to forgive yourself. Although, I don't think you did anything wrong. You stood up for your values and your honor. I admire that." He placed his hands on her shoulders. "Turn it over to God. He'll take the burden off your shoulders."

"I don't think God wants to be bothered with my problems."

"Meg." he pulled her into his arms. "There's no problem, large or small, that God can't help you with."

Tears sprang to her eyes, spilled onto her cheeks and she found herself melting into his comforting embrace. She wanted to believe again, but she just couldn't see how God could help. Her faith had been shaken to the core.

The silence was shattered by Tony's cell phone ringing. He let her go and pulled it from his pocket. "It's Mom." He pushed the talk button "Hi, Mom, what's up?"

She didn't like the look on his face as he listened intently. Something was wrong, she could feel it.

"I'll be right there."

He turned to Meg. "Could you please watch the kids again for a little while? Mom just took Dad to the hospital. She thinks it's just the flu but she wants him checked out by a doctor. He has a history of heart trouble."

"Of course, I'll keep the kids. Here…" She retrieved her car keys from the hook on the wall. "Take the SUV."

He grabbed the keys, kissed her on the cheek then walked to the door. "Kids," he called as he left. "You stay here with Meg and pray for your grandpa. He's in the hospital. He'll be fine," he added quickly, "but he needs your prayers."

Katy took Meg's hand, pulled her toward the couch then knelt down alongside Charlie. The girl put Raggedy Ann beside her. "Kneel down, Meg." Charlie tugged at her free hand. "You heard Dad. Grandpa needs our prayers."

What was she to do? She couldn't tell them she didn't believe God would help so there was nothing to do but kneel. Taking her place between them, she bowed her head and closed her eyes.

While listening to the children ask God to watch over their Grandpa she heard despair in their sweet voices. How could God take their grandfather away from them while they were so young? Something came over her and she found herself whispering, "God, you may not remember me, and I'm not asking anything for myself, but please listen to these precious children as they ask for your healing hand."

Frantic knocking on the door interrupted their prayers. She jumped up, ran over and opened it to see Art and Barbara dressed in their Santa suits, a worried look on both their faces. Was something wrong with them, too?

"We saw Tony take off like a scalded cat in your SUV. What's happening?" Art glanced at the kids.

Barbara walked on into the living room where the children were still kneeling in prayer. She gave Meg an expectant look.

"Tony's mother called him. She has taken his father to the hospital. Could be the flu or could be his heart. She didn't know but wanted him to be checked out." She pointed toward Katy and Charlie. "They're praying for him."

Barbara knelt down beside them and offered her blessing to God and asked for his mercy. Art, in his Santa suit, joined in.

When they all rose, Meg stood beside them. "Do you have time for a cup of coffee?"

"Yes," that would be nice." Barbara followed Meg to the kitchen. "So nice of you to tend to the kids like this."

"It's my pleasure." She realized what she said wasn't token, she meant it. "They've been good for me."

"You've been good for them, too."

"Oh, I don't know, Barbara." She handed the older woman a full cup of coffee. "I didn't mean for them to get so attached. I'll be leaving soon. It just doesn't seem fair to them."

"Don't worry about that, Meg. Tony has explained to them that you will have to go back to New York. I don't think they like the idea, but I'm sure they understand. They just want to spend time with you while you're here." She set her cup down and hugged Meg. "I think their dad might like spending time with you, too."

"Barbara," Meg cautioned, "don't turn into Art, trying to be match-maker."

"I'm just thinking out loud, dear. It's been a sad time for them and you've been like a breath of fresh air. They know you're not going to be here long, but while you're here, it would be nice for them to have some good times. After all, it's Christmas… a time for being merry, decking the halls and most of all, remembering Jesus is the reason for the season." She sat and took a sip of her drink then glanced up at Meg. "It's a time to celebrate His birth and to be joyous. Remember he grew up to be our Lord and Savior who died on the cross to set us free."

Meg turned away. She didn't want the woman to see her tears. "I love you, Barbara…" What was with her teeter-tottering emotions all of a sudden? This was ridiculous. One minute she was angry at God, the next she was a babbling idiot. Crying was something she didn't like to do. "But it's hard for me to be 'joyous' right now."

CHAPTER 7

*B*arbara looked into the other room to see Santa telling the kids Christmas stories.

"Talk to me, Meg. Since Art and I never had kids of our own, you were almost as much ours as you were your parents' child. You could always talk to me when you were young. Why not now?"

Meg hesitated for a long time, wiping her tears away with her hand. "These last few days have made me see what I have been missing in life. I told you I had prayed to God, but he didn't answer. Well, I prayed for a family to love, and being with these kids makes me want it even more. But, and this is a *big* but, I couldn't stay here even if I wanted to."

"And why is that?"

"I don't know how much of my life in New York Mother told you about, but Richard Travis came to my college just before I graduated. He was recruiting girls for his modeling agency. I never wanted to be a model, never gave it a thought, but I went to the audition with my girlfriend to give her support. Richard and his partner Bart Scott talked me into giving it a try."

"Your mother told me some things, but I knew you always wanted to teach."

"I did, but frankly I was so naïve back then I got caught up in their promises of fame and fortune. You know how young women are when someone thinks they're beautiful. I was star struck. I let them talk me into moving to New York." She sighed. "I got booked for a gig , as they call it, right away and made more money than I had ever had in my checking account at one time."

"I can see how a young, beautiful girl could get her head turned by something like that," Barbara told her sympathetically.

"To make a long story short, Richard swept me off my feet. He told me he loved me and I thought we'd marry, have kids, move to Dunsberg…he promised it would all happen someday. After a couple of years, I was miserable with the work I was doing, but it made Richard happy and I wanted him to be happy. Then another year passed. I told him I wanted to get married and start a family. He asked me why I'd want to ruin my figure having babies."

"What a thing to say!" Barbara made a sniffing sound. "I don't think I like that man."

"Anyway, I thought he respected my wishes to— to not—I'm embarrassed to talk about this, but I did not want to give myself to anyone but my husband. He went along with it—never seemed to bother him."

"So?"

"So he ran off with another woman."

Barbara slapped her hand on the table. "Well, that does it. You just stay away from New York. You've been hurt enough."

"I can't," Meg said sadly. "Richard's partner called after I got here and said they were going to sue me for breach of contract."

"Would they do that?"

"Probably. Anyway, I need to go back and take care of that and get out of the lease on my apartment and move on. It's a mess. Richard also took off with some paintings we had purchased together. Pretty expensive stuff. It was stored in my apartment but he had a key."

Barbara thought for a moment, drumming her fingers on the counter top. "My favorite nephew is a top-notch attorney out east. I just may have him check into this Richard Travis. I have a feeling the man's a snake-in-the-grass and my nephew eats those for lunch." She turned and left the kitchen. "Come on Art, I've got a phone call to make before we go to the mall."

****

Tony was a welcomed sight to Meg when he arrived with a smile on his face, a sack full of groceries and clean clothes for the kids.

Charlie ran up to his dad. "How's Grandpa? Did our prayers work?"

"I believe they did. The doctor wants to keep

him for observation for a couple of days, but he assures us he'll be fine. They're pumping him full of antibiotics right now. He was sleeping when I left. Mom's staying with him." He set the grocery bag on the counter.

Meg gave Tony a big hug. "That is wonderful news."

He wrapped his arms around her. "Wow, I may bring you good news more often."

She laughed and her cheeks felt flush. Had she really just done that? She stepped out of his embrace, feeling like an embarrassed school girl. She was thankful for the change of subject.

"Here, I brought food. I'm cooking tonight, if you don't mind."

"My own personal chef. How could I turn that down?" She turned toward the kids. "Is your dad a good cook?"

Charlie looked at Katy and giggled. "He only knows how to cook hotdogs."

"Funny you should say that." Tony started unloading the contents of the sack. "That is exactly what we're having, but tonight we're going to call them gourmet hotdogs."

His kids didn't look that all enthused, so Meg told them, "I could make some macaroni and cheese to go along with those gourmet hotdogs."

Katy Leaped and jumped. "Charlie, she makes macaroni and cheese!"

"Okay, you guys, that's enough insulting me. Here." Tony pulled clothing out of another bag. "Go take a bath and put these clean clothes on."

"I'll go get them started," Meg offered. "Who's

first?"

Katy raised her hand and skipped along behind Meg. "Can Raggedy take a bath with me?"

"No, she doesn't like to get wet." Meg grabbed up the girl and doll and hugged them as hard as she could. Her heart could explode for the little girl and her brother. She was finding it harder and harder to keep those heart strings from tightening.

Katy hugged Meg back. "Let's have another slumber party tonight."

"Suits me." Meg put the girl down and started the bath water. "But you'll have to ask your dad."

"Oh, goodie, maybe, he'll sleep over, too."

"Mmmmm, I don't know about that." She was thankful an excuse quickly came to mind. "You know how he hates to sleep in his clothes."

****

Meg actually found the chilidogs to be rather delicious. After putting the children to bed, Katy in her room, Charlie in the adjoining room upstairs, sleeping in their clothes again, she and Tony cleaned the kitchen.. "I guess. I'll have to admit, though, your macaroni was a bigger hit with the kids."

"You're just being kind."

He took her hand. "Thanks for letting the kids stay over again. They are going to absolutely love living here."

His large hand engulfed hers. She liked the way his touch warmed her heart. "I always loved it. I thought I'd raise my own kids here—" She dropped his hand and tried to step away, but he didn't let her. "Sorry, sore subject."

He pulled her into his arms. "Katy said you prayed for dad."

"I did. Don't know if God recognized my voice."

"Oh, he recognizes all voices. His grace is with us in all times of need."

"Mom used to say that."

"She was right." He pushed away from her so he could look into her face. "Meg, I know you've been hurt, but don't shy away from those who care about you. You have such a good heart. I can see that with my kids."

"Your kids are easy to love. I just don't want to hurt them by leaving, but I have to." She didn't want to look at him. Those big brown eyes would hypnotize her and she didn't need that to happen.

"I know, but let the three of us spend these next few days with you as much as we can. We can help you pack the rest of what you need to take with you, not to mention you'll make our Christmas so special."

Another tug…her heart was becoming entwined, not only with the children, but with the man. "Oh, Tony, I don't know." She shook her head. "I don't know what to say." The touch of his finger under her chin was gentle as he tilted her head back and forced her to meet his gaze.

"Say yes."

What was happening to her? She knew she shouldn't, but she couldn't help but give him an affirmative nod. His bright smile made her happy.

"You'll be doing me a big favor you know."

"How's that?"

"By letting the kids stay here while Dad's in the hospital. I have my visitation day tomorrow and my rounds at the nursing home. Then in the afternoon we have rehearsal for the Christmas program. The kids need to be there. It's the nativity scene but I'm having the kids at church be a big part of it."

What was she getting herself into? It was too late to back out now, and she wasn't really sure she wanted to. "Glad to help out." He threw his head back and laughed. She loved the way it echoed through the house.

Tony met Meg's gaze once again. "Katy will tell you she is going to be a bear."

"A bear?"

"She's a bearer of gifts for baby Jesus, but she thinks it's a bear."

Meg laughed. Kids were special. "That's so cute!"

"Charlie's one of the wise men...the short one."

She laughed again. "They are so precious!"

"Yes, they are," he said quietly, cupping her face in his hands. "And so are you."

She gazed back at his mesmerizing eyes. After a long moment, she asked, "Are you going to kiss me or are you just going to stand there?"

"I thought you'd never ask." He bowed his head downward. "Why don't you meet me half way?" He still didn't make his move.

"What are you doing?"

"Waiting for you."

"I hate you."

"You do not."

"Do, too."

"Do not."

"Okay, I don't. You win." She stood on tip toes and raised her head to meet his lips with hers.

She heard murmurs and was amazed they were coming from her. She had never in her life been kissed with such caring. He brushed his lips softly across hers, whispering against them. "You feel so good, Meg."

"Mmmmm, you feel pretty good yourself, preacher man."

He led her to the couch where they sat close together with his arm around her shoulders. "Tell me more about that *major crush* you had for me in high school."

"I think the basketball uniform had something to do with it," she said jokingly.

"Guess I'm going to have to dig those shorts and tank top out of the mothballs if I'm going to have any allure to you."

Now he was toying with her and she loved it. "I think they might have lost some of their 'allure' after all these years."

"Oh, I don't know." He made a muscle with his free arm. "I work out quite a bit—once or twice a week."

She raised one eyebrow, questioning him.

"Okay, once or twice a month?"

The way he made a question out of what he'd said made her smile. "I think I remember one of the Commandments to say, thou shalt not tell a lie."

"Okay, I don't work out anymore, but I play rough-house with the kids and if you don't think that is a workout—"

She stopped him by kissing him again. "You're perfect just the way you are." Then added playfully, "I don't care what others say."

"Why you little…" He pushed her down on the couch and pinned her arms over her head. "Take that back."

"Okay, you're not perfect just the way you are."

"That's not what I meant and you know it."

His voice softened as he gazed into her eyes. She melted at his playfulness, and yes, she would definitely smile for a week.

"I need to go." He stood up and helped Meg to a sitting position.

"You could have a slumber party and sleep on the couch in your clothes," she teased.

"You know, that's not a bad idea.'

She sat up straight. "I was just kidding."

"I know, but I'm still driving your car and I need to get home to mine. If I stay here tonight, I can catch a ride with Art tomorrow morning. He can drop me off at my house on his way to the mall."

"Logical, but what will people think?"

"When they see my rumpled clothes, they'll think I had a slumber party at a friend's house."

They both laughed as he kicked off his shoes. "Goodnight, friend," he said as he pulled the coverlet that was on the back of the couch over him and closing one eye.

"You're winking at me."

"Am not."

"Are too."

"Are you going to kiss me goodnight?" he

teased.

"No."

"You want to."

"Do not."

"Do too."

She turned, giggling and ran up the stairs.

"I could catch you if I wanted to."

"No you couldn't." She felt like she was fifteen again.

His deep, soothing, *teasing* voice was the last thing she heard before closing the door to her bedroom.

"Could too."

CHAPTER 8

*E*arly the next morning, after having a piece of toast and cup of coffee with him, Meg waved goodbye to Tony. The kids weren't up yet and she was glad she didn't have to explain their dad sleeping over.

Her face seemed to be in a perpetual smile after last night's frolicking with Tony. They were like a couple of kids teasing each other. She had not had so much fun in years. She needed some happiness in her life. What she'd been doing the last few days made her New York troubles seem so far away. She only wished it could last.

Tiny feet scampering down the stairs halted her thoughts. She turned to see little Katy with a huge smile on her face, hair all messed up and cute as a button.

"Meg, we had another slumber party!"

"I know, sweetie. I loved it."

"So did Raggedy."

"I'm sure she did." She watched the little boy make his way down the stairs while he rubbed his eyes. "How about you, Charlie?"

The boy yawned and took the last step. "Can you have a slumber party and not sleep in your clothes? My shirt made me itch all night."

"Tell you what," Meg ruffled his dark hair. "If it's okay with your dad, you could bring your pajamas and some of your clothes and toys here to have when you want to sleep over. After all, this is going to be your home in a few days, and I'd love to have you any time you want to stay. At least until your grandpa gets better."

Both children yelled, "Yea!" and ran to hug her so tight she could barely breathe.

"What would you like for breakfast? Cereal and juice?"

She watched them nod and take their places at the table, along with Raggedy Ann.

Charlie rolled his eyes at Katy. "You know that doll can't eat, don't you."

Katy kissed Raggedy on the cheek. "Then why did Meg give her a little plate yesterday? Besides, even if she can't really eat, she likes to watch."

Meg smiled as tears stung her eyes. Every second with these children made her love them more and made her long for the life she thought she would have by now. Could she love her own children any more than she did Katy and Charlie? She didn't think so.

The doorbell rang. "I'll get it." Katy ran to the door then opened it. "Oh, goody, it's Mrs. Santa."

"Barbara?" Meg poured an extra glass of juice.

"Why aren't you with Art?"

"I'm meeting him later. He went with Tony to the nursing home to hand out gifts to the shut-ins."

"They'll love that." She handed the glass to the older woman.

"Thank you." She took a sip. "Ahh, that hits the spot. I just wanted to let you know I talked to my attorney nephew. He's getting right on the Richard Travis thing. So if you get a call from a Theodore Crowley, you'll know who it is."

"He's probably a busy man, Barbara, I hate to take his time."

"He said this was right up his alley and he's glad to do it."

Charlie was rapt with curiosity while they spoke. "What's a Richard Travis thing?"

Barbara patted him on the head. "It's grown-up stuff. Nothing for you to worry about."

Katy finished the last drop of her juice. "Ask Dad. He knows lots of things."

Meg picked up Katy's empty glass. She couldn't have the kids talking to Tony about this. "No, no, no, don't bother your dad."

Barbara whispered to Meg, "Sorry. Little pitchers have big ears. Wasn't thinking." She turned toward the door. "Thanks for the juice. I'll let myself out. You kids be good for Meg."

"They're always good. Bye Barbara, have a good day." Meg watched her friend close the door then faced the children. "How would you like to see the tree house?" She smiled when Charlie's eyes got as big as saucers.

"Could we?" She reached for a pan, filled it with

water and placed it on the stove. "It's cold, but I think if I make a big thermos of hot chocolate and we put on our coats, hats, scarves and gloves, we'll be okay as long as the chocolate lasts."

****

She took along a blanket just in case, but it was snug and cozy up in the tree house after a while. Many good memories were made in that old tree house. She'd have to thank Art for fixing it up. Matter of fact, she didn't remember thanking him for anything he'd done. That would have to be fixed.

Pouring the hot chocolate, she listened to the children recite their parts in the Christmas pageant they would be rehearsing later. Meg held back giggling out loud at Charlie's rendition of a wise man in a much deeper voice than was comfortable for him; and Katy's *bear* pretending to hand out gifts to a baby Jesus lasted a good ten minutes. Meg doubted she could actually carry that many gifts in her tiny arms on the night of the performance.

Time had passed so fast she hadn't realized they'd been out so long until Katy's eyes began to sleepily droop. "Maybe we should go in for a sandwich and then a nap before your dad comes to pick you up?" She was pleased when they agreed.

****

"Dad," Katy squealed when he came in the door that afternoon, "we had hot chocolate in the tree house."

"Wow." Tony picked her up, twirled her around then put her down again. "Wish I'd have been here."

Charlie hugged his dad around the waist "I don't think there would have been enough room for all four of us."

"Oh, I think we could have made room." Tony cocked one eyebrow at Meg. "You could sit on my lap."

Charlie wrinkled his nose. "Ewwww, mushy stuff."

"Get back to me in a few years, Son. I think you'll change your tune."

Katy giggled and Meg shook her head. "No one is sitting on anyone's lap in the tree house. Now get going. You'll be late for rehearsal."

"Aren't you coming with us?" Tony helped Katy with her coat.

"No, I have things I need to do. I'd like to give a party before I leave town and I need to do some shopping."

"When's the party?"

"After your dad gets out of the hospital, and when I can get everyone together on a night they're not busy. You remember Brian Stokes?"

"Sure, I see him and his family every Sunday at church. In fact, their baby is going to be baby Jesus in the Christmas program."

"Well, I rented the SUV from him and promised to meet his wife and kids, so I thought I'd invite them, your folks, you and the kids, of course, and last but certainly not least, Santa and his Mrs."

"Sounds like a lot of work. Anything I can do?"

"Be there or be square."

Katy fell into a fit of giggles again. "Be there or be square, Dad," she repeated.

Tony glanced at his daughter and smiled. "Do you even know what that means?"

The child shook her head. "No, but it sounds like it's supposed to be funny."

"You're so smart!" Meg hugged Katy then turned her attention to Tony. "Oh, another thing, Tony. Why don't you bring the kids back here for the night? Bring their pajamas, a few changes of clothes and anything else they would want to have here. Like I told them, this is going to be their home soon and if they want to move their things in early, it's fine with me." Tony gave her one of those devastating grins and butterflies invaded her heart.

"What about their dad?"

She took hold of his shoulders and turned him toward the door. "Their dad is leaving right now."

She kissed the children goodbye. "Do good. See you later."

****

Meg made her grocery list and other essentials to buy for the party. It would be her last hurrah in Dunsberg, and she wanted to go out on a happy note. It might well be her last bit of happiness for a long time.

Oh, well, she wasn't going to think about that. She wanted to keep the joyful feelings she had at the moment. There would be plenty of time to ponder the rest of her life after she left, but for now, she couldn't stop smiling.

She marveled at how friendly people were in her small hometown. No pushing or shoving in stores and no ugly words coming out of people's mouths. Every clerk took time to be helpful and some remembered her as a young girl and told humorous childhood stories on others she knew.

By the time she got home with her wares and had put them away, she wanted only to collapse on the couch in front of a warm fire. She remembered the logs Art had piled on her porch and brought in a few. After crumpling up some of her grocery bags and laying the smaller logs on top of the paper, she soon saw a few embers spitting upward and added a couple larger logs. A full-fledged fire soon glowed. She only wished Tony and the kids were there to enjoy it with her.

CHAPTER 9

Meg didn't remember falling asleep, but woke to the sound of the doorbell. The clock told her she had been asleep over an hour. Rubbing her eyes, she opened the door to three smiling faces. Tony, Katy and Charlie all held suitcases and shopping bags with boxes of toys under their arms.

Tony met her gaze and shrugged. "Don't say it, if you don't mean it."

Meg loved the way his eyes smiled. "I meant it." She stepped aside so they could come inside. "Kids, put your things in your rooms. Have you had supper?"

"We brought supper."

"Hot dogs again?"

Tony held up one of the bags. "Nope. It's a surprise."

The children scampered up the stairs with their things while Meg took the sack of food to the kitchen. She peeked in the sack and instantly realized she was hungry. "Chinese Carryout? I didn't even know Dunsberg had a Chinese restaurant."

"It's new," Tony said from the living room. "Pretty good. If you don't like Chinese, I'll be glad to go out for something else."

"What, are you nuts? I love Chinese!" She unloaded the cartons from the bag, got out some paper plates and utensils then joined him in the living room. He stood in front of the fire with his hands in his pockets looking captivated. God he was handsome.

When she walked up beside him, he pulled his hands free, reached for her then put his arm around her shoulders. "Now this is what I'm talking about."

She met his gaze and the reflection of the fire flickered in them. Her breath caught in her throat when he tipped her chin up with one finger and kissed her. Softly at first and then with more intensity and she welcomed it. Her will power completely gone, she kissed him back while wrapping her arms around his neck.

What was she doing, she didn't know but she liked the way this man made her feel. However, this was insane. She couldn't get wrapped up in his world. His lips released her and she stepped away, then tried to make light of what had happened with a chuckle. "Ewwww, mushy stuff."

"Mushy's my middle name." He pulled her back into his arms.

"You're goofy."

"That's my last name."

Why couldn't she stop herself from leaning into

his embrace? "Hmmm, Tony Mushy Goofy. Has a ring to it." Her eyes never left his, and she was unsure about the serious way he looked at her.

"Goofy's what happens to a man when he feels he's falling in love."

No, please, no! She whirled away and turned her back to him. "Tony, don't."

"Meg."

He gently touched her arm and she was relieved he didn't try to force her to face him. "Please, Tony, I can't—"

"I'm not asking you to say you're falling for me. I don't want anything from you except to spend time with you while I can. But I do want you to know I haven't felt this alive for a long time. Truthfully, I never thought I'd feel this way again."

The sincerity in his voice threatened to break down her defenses, but she couldn't allow that. "You know this will end in heartbreak."

"No, I don't, and neither do you. I will tell you assuredly, God has a plan. I can feel it in my bones. All you need to do is open your aching heart and let love in."

"I-it's not that easy." Welcomed chatter from the children came in time to stop her from bursting into tears. She tried to make her voice sound cheery. "What is that you have there?"

They had a board game they wanted them all to play. It was a bible verse game. Meg's shoulders dropped. She just couldn't get away from bibles, church, God. Could they be right? Was God always there?

****

She arose early the morning of the party. The children had stayed at their grandparents' house the night before since they hadn't seen much of their grandpa, and she welcomed the quiet time.

The aroma of fresh brewed coffee filled the house. She got a cup, grabbed her mother's recipe box and headed for the couch. When she sat down and got comfortable, she allowed her mind to trace the happenings of the last few days which had passed quickly.

Mr. Stenbrook had left the hospital in good health. Katy and Charlie stayed with her for the most part and Tony came and went, but never brought up the subject of love again. He only referenced it once, to say that if it was God's will, it would be. She'd known what he was talking about, but chose to ignore it.

He still gave her warm embraces from time to time, but she had to admit she missed his kisses. It was hard for her to let go of what they had started to share, but she could only blame herself. She constantly fought her emotions. Her feelings for Tony were—

She sat up, leaned forward and noticed her hands trembled when she placed her cup on the coffee table. "Oh, no. Are you falling in love?" No, she couldn't be. She was comfortable with Tony and the kids that was all. Temporarily pretending to have a loving family wasn't a bad thing.

Pretending? Or was it real? Falling in love? Or not? Staying or going…it all blurred together. She didn't know what to think anymore. She did know, right now New York was a million miles away.

She relaxed back. Now wasn't the time to be philosophizing her life. She had a party to give. Willing herself to be calm, she picked up the recipe box and placed it in her lap.

Smiling, she read the notes her mother had made on the margins of the recipes as she thumbed through the box. "Yum!" was written on the corn casserole recipe so she laid it aside to make. The yeast rolls read, "Irresistible," so that went in the to-do pile. She thought of making her own pot roast with potatoes and onions that she had made numerous times with great success.

When she came across the pecan pie recipe, the note written on the top caught her eye. *He proposed after eating this pie.* Meg knew her mom meant her father. Then she suddenly remembered Charlie telling Santa at the mall the first day she saw him that his dad could eat his weight in pecan pie.

"Hmmm, should I or shouldn't I?" she mumbled out loud. Should won out. She had planned to use her pecans for homemade candy, but pecan pie seemed to be calling her name. Was it God's will?

****

Barbara was the first to arrive that evening with coleslaw and a veggie tray. "Santa will be along later to surprise the kids." She laughed. "Big surprise. They know Art's Santa but they actually think he's the real Santa anyway."

Meg took the veggie tray and led the way to the

kitchen. "He is, isn't he?"

"He's been *my* Santa for over fifty years." Barbara sighed.

"I envy you."

"Not too late for you to have the same happiness."

"How do you mend a broken heart, Mrs. Claus?" Barbara put the slaw down and held out her arms for a hug. Meg willingly went to her.

"I know three people who would be the best glue to put that heart back together again. Katy and Charlie, but mostly Tony."

"I don't know, Barbara. I don't think I can. I don't want to hurt anyone."

"How could you possibly hurt anyone?"

"I'm afraid it would be hard for me to trust again. Those three don't deserve that." The words *God's will,* kept poking at the back of her mind.

When Meg's cell phone rang she picked it up and looked at the caller ID. "It's your nephew, Theodore."

"I call him Teddy."

"Well, you know him a little better than I do." She smiled at the woman she admired so much and flipped the phone open.

"Hello, this is Meg Stanley.

"Yes. Yes, I understand. I so appreciate it.

"No, really, I can't thank you enough.

"Yes, I'll let you know when I receive it.

" Okay, and please send me your statement.

Meg couldn't believe what she was hearing. "What? No, I won't hear of you doing it for nothing."

She glanced over at Barbara with a scolding look. "Oh, you're doing it for your favorite aunt?" Meg couldn't be angry, she smiled at Barbara. "She happens to be my favorite person, too, and she's standing right beside me as we speak... Yes, you may talk to her." She handed the phone to the older woman.

"Ah, Teddy, I guess it's good news. You're the greatest. Wish you were here. We're having a party tonight.... Okay, maybe Easter. Love you." She handed the phone back to Meg. "Problem solved?"

"Part of it." She closed her cell phone. "I'm supposed to get a sizeable check from Richard for my half of the sale of the paintings. It's being sent to your address since, according to Teddy, you're my local representative."

"Wow, I got a promotion from Mrs. Santa to *local representative*. I'm impressed!"

They were still laughing when Tony and the kids arrived. Meg walked toward the door. "I wonder how Mr. Travis is going to feel when he gets hit with the court order to pay up."

"I'd like to be a fly on the wall when it happens."

She opened the door, gave the kids a hug and patted Tony on the cheek then looked back at Barbara. "I don't know how your nephew did it and I don't care how. He did it. That's all that counts. He also said I should be hearing from Travis-Scott Agency about the contract and to let him know if that doesn't go the way I want it to."

"What's this all about?" Tony hung his coat on the rack.

"It's a long story, but it's settled. Let's not spoil

the party." Meg didn't want anything to get in the way of an evening of happiness. *If it's God's will.*

CHAPTER 10

$\mathcal{M}$eg watched Charlie out of the corner of her eye as he approached his dad. The boy was up to something and she hoped he wasn't about to tell Tony what she thought he was. He seemed to be trying to act more grown up than he was. Yep, there it was.

"It's probably that Richard Travis thing."

She rushed to Charlie, and pulled him to her side. "You're dad doesn't know about that. Let's not bother him with it, okay?" Tony eyed her with a serious stare. She had never seen him look like that. His voice was even more somber.

"I know who Richard Travis is."

She glanced at Barbara, who had a puzzled look, and then looked back at Tony. "You do?"

"Art told me."

Barbara turned to Meg. The total look of horror on the woman's face almost made her laugh.

"I'm sorry. I told Art about our conversation the

other day when I called Teddy for help. I told the old codger to keep it to himself."

"Buuuut?" Meg fought back the smile that almost escaped when Barbara held her hands up in submission.

"But, you know Art. If you want news to travel, tell the man. He spreads gossip faster than a wild fire…N-no, faster than facebook, or e-mail, maybe even telephone or telegraph, and that twitter and tweeting thing I hear about." She dropped her hands as if surrendering to the unknown. "Whatever that is."

Meg couldn't help it, she had to laugh at the reference to social media. "It's okay, Barbara." She glanced at Tony with, what she hoped was, a reassuring look. "The problem is settled. Most of it anyway."

She jumped at the sound of her cell phone. Thankful for the interruption; that is until she looked at the caller ID. "Charlie and Katy, go upstairs and play for a while, would you please?" When they left the room, she turned her attention to Tony and Barbara. "It's Richard. I'm putting him on speaker. I don't seem to have any secrets anymore, and if I can't trust you two, who can I trust?" Had she really just said that? Was she beginning to trust again?

She flipped open her phone and pushed the 'speaker on' button. "Hello."

"Meg, it's good to hear you voice, babe."

Tony winced and shook his head. She didn't recognize the look on the handsome man's face. He obviously didn't like Richard calling her babe.

Neither did she. "I'm not your 'babe'."

"Hey, I know I made a big mistake, and I want to make it up to you. I should have never left the way I did."

"Which way was that? The way you left with Cynthia or the way you left with the paintings?" She knew anything that came out of his mouth would be a lie.

"Yeah, well, about the paintings. We bought those for an investment."

He was such a jerk! How could she have been so blind? "Let me stop you right there. We bought them for our future home."

"But, I had an opportunity to sell them for a sizeable profit. I planned to send you half."

"Tell me, did you plan that before or after my attorney contacted you?"

"Babe...ah-er, Meg, that's another thing. You didn't need to sic some shyster lawyer—"

Meg could tell that reference ruffled Barbara's feathers big time. The woman started to grab the phone, but Meg shook her head and gently grabbed her friend's hand to stop her.

"Be grateful, Richard. I could have filed charges, but I didn't. Think about it, you went into my apartment, without my permission, and took the paintings. That's theft in anyone's book. Now, I believe our conversation's over...unless you have something to say about letting me out of my contract with the agency." Seconds went by before she heard his voice again. She could almost feel him squirm. He deserved it.

"That's something else I wanted to talk to you

about." He took a deep breath. "I know we're through as a couple. I screwed up, I'll admit that, but that shouldn't keep us from having a professional arrangement. Bart had no business talking to you the way he did. You're our top model, ba-- sorry. You're the one all the clients ask for. Come back, Meg. We can work things out, at least at the office."

She refused to fall into his *business only* trap. "There's nothing to work out, Richard. I don't want to work for you anymore. I'm asking you let me out of the contract. No, I'm telling you. If you don't, I'll have to sic my *shyster lawyer* on you again." She glanced at Barbara, and this time at the reference, the woman smiled.

"Meg, be reasonable. We need you. We made you what you are today. You need us! Losing you will cost you *and* us a lot of money."

What she was today? Oh, yeah, a woman who'd been manipulated like a puppet with Richard pulling the strings, taken advantage of, used for her looks and left with a broken heart.

"Ah, the money. It's always the money, isn't it, Richard." She took a calming breath and refused to let him get the upper hand. "Do I need to have my lawyer contact you for a dissolution agreement?"

"Meg, I don't think you're realizing the income you're giving up."

She didn't care about her income, but she knew Richard was realizing his percentage was going down the drain. "My attorney will be getting in touch—"

"Okay, you win. I don't want him poking around

in my business." His tone turned surly. "You must be crazy to give up what you had here."

She thought about his words and knew in her heart immediately what she wanted to say. "No, I'd be crazy to give up all I have *here*. Goodbye, Richard."

Slowly she closed the cell phone, smiled at Barbara then walked over to the very solemn Tony. Reaching up, she entwined her fingers into the back of his hair, then pulled his face towards hers. She thought she saw a glint of realization in his beautiful brown eyes just before they closed and her lips met his with a long, hard kiss that almost took her breath. The world around them disappeared until Barbara cleared her throat. Reluctantly, she ended the kiss and glanced at her friend.

"I'm proud of you," Barbara said. "Not just for what you said to that jerk, but that kiss. Wow! That was a doozy! Wait until I tell Santa."

Tony and Meg both looked her square in the eye and said in unison, "Don't!"

****

The party was a huge success. Brian's wife was someone she thought could be her best friend, their older children had a blast entertaining Charlie and Katy, and the baby was adorable. Meg couldn't wait to see the Christmas program with the baby as a real live Jesus in the manger.

Art. Oh how she loved the man, and the way his eyes shined with glee when he passed out his bag of gifts and candy. It made her all warm and fuzzy inside. When she looked around the room at her friends and loved ones, her heart nearly burst with love.

Suddenly, a heavy burden lifted from her shoulders and she felt a peace she hadn't felt for a really long time. She knew she could now love and be loved with an open, pure heart. *Oh, God, thank you. I owe You the glory.*

Everyone seemed delighted with his or her presents. Mrs. Stenbrook loved the scarf and gloves from Tony. However, she seemed especially charmed with the musical card Meg had the kids make for her. They had recorded their own voices on it, and tried to make it very special. When Mrs. Stenbrook opened it and heard Katy and Charlie singing, *Jesus Loves Me* ending with *Merry Christmas, Grandma, we love you*, then wiped a tear from her eye, Meg realized it was the perfect gift.

Meg knew Tony was touched by her gift to him…a gold key chain that she had engraved: "1 Corinthians, 13:13", which she knew he knew it meant basically that three things will last forever…faith, hope, and love…the greatest of these is love.

She was truly believing again that love would prevail.

****

Singing of Christmas carols until they were hoarse rounded out the evening. As the festivities died down, Meg fondled the heart-shaped locket around her neck. It was her gift from Katy and Charlie and it had their crookedly cut pictures in it. She would cherish it forever, just as she would them.

"This was great, Megan," Brian said, bundling up his sleepy kids while his wife wrapped a blanket around the baby.

"Perfect," said Mr. Stenbrook. "I loved the meal." He patted his belly. "Much, much better than hospital food."

They all seemed to agree as she watched her friends walk out into the chilly night. The contentment she felt as she closed the door was something she'd never experienced before. She glanced at the sleepy little girl and boy on the couch, then heard Tony's voice and turned toward him.

"I thought they'd never leave." He pulled a small box out of his pocket. "I wanted to give you this while we were alone." He looked toward his kids. "Well, semi-alone, anyway."

Her knees threatened to buckle when the man of her dreams got down on one knee and gazed up at her. This couldn't be happening! Was her heart going to beat right out of her chest?

Tony opened the box, removed the beautiful diamond engagement ring and held it out to her. Surely she was going to swoon at his next words.

"Will you marry me?"

She didn't have to say a word, she knew her eyes screamed, "Yes, yes, yes!"

He stood, slipped the ring on her finger then his lips brushed hers before he spoke. "I was thinking,

New York's a nice place to visit, but I wouldn't want to live there, so why don't we go there, take in a Broadway show or something. I mean, that way we could take care of the lease on your apartment and make arrangements to have your belongings shipped back home."

Home. It was the most beautiful place in the world. She fumbled with the buttons on his shirt; sure her happiness would spill onto the floor any minute. "Wouldn't be much to ship. The apartment came furnished so it's only clothes and personal stuff—but it can wait. We have a wedding to plan."

"Mmmm, yes, there's that, but right now I'm wondering if I could have another kiss like you gave me earlier in front of Barbara...or maybe another piece of pecan pie...whichever you'd rather."

"How about both." She kissed him, and their mouths formed a grin when they heard Charlie.

"Ewwww! Yuk! Too much mushy stuff."

****

The check and papers dissolving Meg of any further business with Travis-Scott Agency arrived special delivery. All was right with the world, and that made her happy. She helped get Katy and Charlie dressed in their costumes for their big night. "You're going to be fantastic," she told them, kissing their rosy cheeks. Tony arrived right on time to take them to the church, and as always, he was as handsome as could be. Her heart soared with pride just knowing she would soon be his bride.

The Christmas program was a big hit. Naturally, Meg thought Katy and Charlie were the cutest of all the children. The best part was when baby Jesus started to cry really loud. Her heart filled with pride when Katy walked over and placed Raggedy Ann in the crib and said sweetly.

"Don't cry, baby Jesus. My dolly friend will lay with you so you won't be scared."

When the baby suddenly stopped crying and cooed with delight, the applause was deafening. Tears welled in Meg's eyes and spilled onto her cheeks at the precious moment. However, the highlight of the evening was when Barbara, in her beautiful soprano voice, sang *O Holy Night*. Not only Meg, but everyone in the church wept at the beauty of it.

Meg bowed her head in whispered prayer. "Please God, forgive me. I walked away from You, but You never walked away from me. I promise never ever to forsake You again. I thought You didn't answer my prayers when all along You did. You knew what was right for me. Barbara said You would grant me what I needed. I needed a family and someone to love. If it's Your will, I will love this family you have given me with all my heart, as long as I live. Thank you, Lord. Amen."

The warmth of Tony's hand on her back penetrated her blouse. She met his gaze and saw love in his eyes when he spoke.

"I couldn't help but overhear you. Does this mean…?"

She looked down. "I'm goofy," she stated honestly.

"No, I'm goofy."

"No you're not. I am."

"Are not."

"Am too."

"Not."

"Too."

He placed his finger under her chin and tilted her head upward. "Hey, remember? My last name's goofy."

The comical, superior look on his face made her want to laugh.

He puffed his chest out. "Just think, soon you'll be Mrs. Goofy."

She loved this man more than life itself. "I can't wait." She cherished his kids, too, and was thrilled to be a part of their lives forever.

****

The four of them stood before the fireplace Christmas evening hand in hand and said a prayer of thanks for all their blessings.

"This has been One Special Christmas," Meg said, hugging the children to her.

"And many more to come," Tony added just before he leaned down to kiss her and placing his hand over Charlie's mouth to muffle, "Ewwwwwwwwwwwwww."

About the Author

Norma Eaton is author of a full-length romance novel, magazine articles and short stories. She was a long time member of Ozarks Romance Authors as well as other writing groups. She and her husband sing gospel in and around Branson, MO. and reside in Springfield, MO. She thanks God for giving her the joy of writing.